PINGU

BBC CHILDREN'S BOOKS

Pingu admires Pingo's new skis.

Pingo lets him stand on the back.

Planks make good skis too.

Pingu quickly makes his own skis.

He climbs the hill.

Pingo shows Pingu how to ski.

But Pingu goes slowly.

ingu thinks Pingo is good at skiing.

But Pingo went too fast.

Pingu slides down carefully.

"Watch out," says Pingo.

Pingu falls into the dip.

The two friends share skis.

PINGU

and

The Sledge Outing

Pingu and his friends go sledging.

It's a hard climb up the hill.

Shall I go on my back or my tummy

Pingu's sledge won't move.

He has to push it.

The runners are rusty.

Pingu cleans off the rust.

Now he is the fastest.

But the sledge crashes into the ice.

Pingu is inside the snowman.

His friends take Pingu home.

The snowman melts.

Pingu and his friends have a good lau